P9-BXV-441

E BEN
Benjamin, A. H.
It could have been worse

2/06

DEMCO

THIS LITTLE TIGER BOOK BELONGS TO:

_____

_____

_____

_____

This edition published 1999
First published in the United States 1998 by
Little Tiger Press, N16 W23390 Stoneridge Drive, Waukesha, W1 53188
Originally published in Great Britain 1998 by Magi Publications, London
Text © 1998 A. H. Benjamin · Illustrations © 1998 Tim Warnes

All rights reserved

Library of Congress Cataloging-in-Publication Data
Benjamin, A. H. , 1950-
It could have been worse / by A. H. Benjamin; illustrated by Tim Warnes.
p.   cm.
Summary: While walking home, an "unlucky" mouse suffers minor
mishaps which repeatedly save him from being eaten by various animals.
ISBN 1-58431-006-5 (pb)
[1. Mice—Fiction 2. Luck—Fiction.] I. Warnes, Tim,   ill. II. Title.
PZ7.B43457It 1998 [E]—dc21 98-29407 CIP AC
Printed in Belgium
First U.S. paperback edition
1 3 5 7 9 10 8 6 4 2

For Sue and Paul
A.H.B.

For Jess
T.W.

MT. PLEASANT PUBLIC LIBRARY
MT. PLEASANT, IOWA

IT COULD HAVE BEEN WORSE

by A.H. Benjamin

Pictures by Tim Warnes

Mouse was on his way back home
after visiting his town cousin
when . . .

WHOOPS!

he lost his balance
and fell to the ground.

"Ouch!" said Mouse.
"This isn't my lucky
day."

But it could have
been worse!

Mouse picked himself up
and continued on his way.
He came to an open field
and was scurrying across it
when . . .

CRASH!

he fell into a dark hole.

"Why do things *always* go wrong for me?" grumbled Mouse.

But it could have been worse!

Mouse climbed out of the hole and was off again, but soon he got sleepy.

"I think I'll take a rest," Mouse said.
He had just found a comfortable spot
when . . .

OUCH!

he sat on a thistle and
shot into the air.

"Everything bad happens to me!" wailed Mouse as he pulled the thorns out of his fur.

But it could have been worse!

Mouse trotted down the
hill until he reached a stream.
He began to cross it using
the stepping stones
when . . .

SPLASH!

he slipped
and fell.

"I'll catch a cold!"
complained Mouse.

But it could have been worse!

Mouse paddled to the edge of the stream
and climbed out of the water.

Shaking himself dry, he was just
about to scramble down a steep bank
when . . .

WHEEE!

he lost his footing and
skidded to the bottom.

"I'll be black and blue all over," cried Mouse.

But it could have been worse!

Mouse staggered to his feet
and ran the rest of the way home.

"It's been a terrible day," he said to his mother
as she bathed his cuts and bruises. "I fell into a hole,
got wet in the river, and—"

"Never mind, son," she said . . .

All books available from most retailers.
In case of difficulty please contact
Little Tiger Press,
N16 W23390 Stoneridge Drive,
Waukesha, WI 53188
or visit us online: www.futechinteractive.com